Dear Parents,

Welcome to the Scholastic Reader series. We have taken over 80 years of experience with teachers, parents, and children and put it into a program that is designed to match your child's interests and skills.

Level 1—Short sentences and stories made up of words kids can sound out using their phonics skills and words that are important to remember.

Level 2—Longer sentences and stories with words kids need to know and new "big" words that they will want to know.

Level 3—From sentences to paragraphs to longer stories, these books have large "chunks" of texts and are made up of a rich vocabulary.

Level 4—First chapter books with more words and fewer pictures.

It is important that children learn to read well enough to succeed in school and beyond. Here are ideas for reading this book with your child:

- Look at the book together. Encourage your child to read the title and make a prediction about the story.
- Read the book together. Encourage your child to sound out words when appropriate. When your child struggles, you can help by providing the word.
- Encourage your child to retell the story. This is a great way to check for comprehension.
- Have your child take the fluency test on the last page to check progress.

Scholastic Readers are designed to support your child's efforts to learn how to read at every age and every stage. Enjoy helping your child learn to read and love to read.

> **—Francie Alexander**
> Chief Education Officer
> Scholastic Education

For Steve, my very own Math Monster
—G.M.

For Paul III,
who was always good in math
—M.H.

Copyright © 1995 by Scholastic Inc.
The activities on pages 27-32 © 1995 by Marilyn Burns.
Fluency Activities © 2003 Scholastic Inc.

All rights reserved. Published by Scholastic Inc.
SCHOLASTIC, CARTWHEEL BOOKS, and associated logos are trademarks
and/or registered trademarks of Scholastic Inc.

Library of Congress Cataloging-in-Publication Data is available.

ISBN 0-590-22712-2

16 15 14 13 12 11   07 08 09 10 11 12/0

Printed in the U.S.A.   23

First printing, September 1995

MONSTER MATH

by Grace Maccarone
Illustrated by Marge Hartelius
Math Activities by Marilyn Burns

Scholastic Reader — Level 1

Cartwheel
·B·O·O·K·S· ®

SCHOLASTIC INC.
New York Toronto London Auckland Sydney
Mexico City New Delhi Hong Kong Buenos Aires

Twelve little monsters
wake up at seven.

One jogs away.
Now there are . . .

Eleven little monsters
meet in a den.

One sneaks away.
Now there are . . .

Ten little monsters
walk in a line.

One skips away.
Now there are . . .

Nine little monsters
jump over a gate.

One runs away.
Now there are . . .

Eight little monsters
sip tea at eleven.

One strolls away
Now there are . . .

Seven little monsters
are up to monster tricks.

One rolls away.
Now there are . . .

Six little monsters
go for a drive.

One walks away.
Now there are . . .

Five little monsters
dance along the shore.

One swims away.
Now there are . . .

Four little monsters
climb up a tree.

One flies away.
Now there are . . .

Three little monsters
cook a monster stew.

One moves away.
Now there are . . .

Two little monsters
go for a run.

One hops away.
Now there is . . .

One little monster
is a big hero.
It goes home.
Now there are zero!

• ABOUT THE ACTIVITIES •

For children, learning to count is much like learning the alphabet. Both are sequences of sounds learned through repeated practice. You probably can't automatically say the alphabet backwards because no relationships exist among the letters to determine their order. But counting backwards is easy for adults because we've long ago linked number names with the quantities and symbols that represent them. Our understanding has its base in logic.

Young children, however, are not aware of the logic of our number system. When they first learn to count, they usually do not link the names for numbers with the meanings of the numbers. They have not yet learned relationships such as *one fewer* and *one more*. The activities and games in this section will help children develop an understanding of number relationships. Counting backwards then becomes obvious.

Reread the story and encourage your child to predict the number that's coming up. Then try some of these activities. The directions are written for you to read along with your child. Be open to your child's interests and have fun with math!

— Marilyn Burns

You'll find tips and suggestions
for guiding the activities whenever
you see a box like this!

Retelling the Story

Get some counters. You can use pennies, buttons, or beans. You'll also need a small cup that will hold 12 counters.

Make a pile of 12 counters, one for each monster in the book. Count out loud to make sure you have exactly 12. Keep the counters near you. Don't put them in the cup yet.

Now, reread the book. Each time a monster goes away, put one counter in the cup. Each time you do that, guess how many counters are left outside the cup. Count to check.

At the end of the story, ask your child how many counters are inside the cup and how many are outside the cup. Don't be surprised if your child has to count to be sure there are 12 in the cup.

Take Out

Turn the cup upside down. Hide three counters underneath. Now reach in and take out just one counter. Put it on top of the cup. How many counters are left under the cup? Guess first, then lift the cup to check.

Now play again, but hide four counters underneath the cup. Take out just one and put it on top. How many are left underneath? Lift the cup to check. Then try with other numbers you choose.

Show Me

For this game, you call out the number, and your child shows it with counters. Choose numbers so that sometimes your child needs to take out more counters and sometimes needs to put counters back into the cup. Your child might put all the counters back into the cup and start over for each number, or may just take or return additional counters as needed. Don't show your child a way you think is easier; just observe how he or she is thinking.

Start with all the counters in the cup. Say a number from 1 to 10. Take that many counters out of the cup. Count to be sure you have the right amount. Put each counter in a square and leave the rest in the cup.

Now say another number. Change what's on the board so you show the new number of counters.

Keep saying other numbers and changing the counters.

One More

This game is like *Take Out*, but here you hide counters under the cup instead of taking any out. Start with zero counters under the cup. Then lift the cup and slide one under. How many are there under the cup? Lift the cup and count to check.

Slide one more counter under the cup. Now how many are under there?

Keep going until all of the counters are hidden under the cup.

Two More

This is a harder game. Play it the same way you play *One More*. Start with zero counters under the cup. Each time, put in two counters, then guess how many are in the cup. Count to check.

For *Two More,* your child may not predict correctly. Counting to check helps him or her begin to learn the pattern of counting by 2's.